save the . . .
GIRAFFES

by **Anita Sanchez**
with an introduction
by **Chelsea Clinton**

PHILOMEL

This book is respectfully dedicated to
Dr. Anne Innis Dagg, the very first giraffologist.

PHILOMEL BOOKS
An imprint of Penguin Random House LLC, New York

First published in the United States of America by Philomel Books,
an imprint of Penguin Random House LLC, 2023

Visit us online at penguinrandomhouse.com.

Library of Congress Cataloging-in-Publication Data is available.

Printed in the United States of America

ISBN 9780593404171 (hardcover)
ISBN 9780593404188 (paperback)

1st Printing

LSCC

Edited by Talia Benamy and Jill Santopolo
Design by Lily Qian
Text set in Calisto MT Pro

save the . . .

save the . . .
BLUE WHALES

save the . . .
ELEPHANTS

save the . . .
FROGS

save the . . .
GIRAFFES

save the . . .
GORILLAS

save the . . .
LIONS

save the . . .
POLAR BEARS

save the . . .
TIGERS

save the . . .
WHALE SHARKS

Dear Reader,

When I was around your age, my favorite animals were dinosaurs and elephants. I wanted to know everything I could about triceratopses, stegosauruses and other dinosaurs that had roamed our earth millions of years ago. Elephants, though, captured my curiosity and my heart. The more I learned about the largest animals on land today, the more I wanted to do to help keep them and other endangered species safe forever.

So I joined organizations working around the world to support endangered species and went to our local zoo to learn more about conservation efforts close to home (thanks to my parents and grandparents). I tried to learn as much as I could about how we can ensure animals and plants don't go extinct like the dinosaurs, especially since it's the choices that we're making that pose the greatest threat to their lives today.

The choices we make don't have to be huge to make

a real difference. When I was in elementary school, I used to cut up the plastic rings around six-packs of soda, glue them to brightly colored construction paper (purple was my favorite) and hand them out to whomever would take one in a one-girl campaign to raise awareness about the dangers that plastic six-pack rings posed to marine wildlife around the world. I learned about that from a book—*50 Simple Things Kids Can Do to Save the Earth*—which helped me understand that you're never too young to make a difference and that we all can change the world. I hope that this book will inform and inspire you to help save this and other endangered species. There are tens of thousands of species that are currently under threat, with more added every year. We have the power to save those species, and with your help, we can.

Sincerely,

Chelsea Clinton

save the . . .
GIRAFFES

CONTENTS

1

MEET THE GIRAFFES

If you want to look a giraffe in the eye, you have to look up . . . up . . . up! The giraffe looms high over your head, calmly chewing leaves while its keen, long-lashed eyes gaze down at you standing far below. Giraffes are the tallest animals in the world. An adult giraffe can be more than seventeen feet tall—that's about as high as three six-foot humans balancing on each other's shoulders.

Most of us, if we're lucky enough to see a live

Giraffes have best friends just like people do!

giraffe, watch them in a human-created environment. Giraffes have been kept in zoos for a very, very long time. Thousands of years ago, Egyptian pharaohs sent expeditions south of the Sahara Desert to capture these strange-looking creatures. Roman emperors prized them to use in victory parades. From ancient times, the earliest scientists were mystified by giraffes. Ancient Chinese explorers thought they looked like a kind of unicorn. Some Greek naturalists had a theory they were a cross between a long-necked camel and a leopard. Century after century, people marveled at these unique animals in zoos all over the world.

But in the wild, giraffes live in a very different habitat from a crowded urban zoo. Giraffes live on the continent of Africa (an enormous land mass three times the size of the United States) and they're found in many African countries. These majestic animals roam a habitat called the savanna. A savanna is a grassland that has warm temperatures all year long and is dotted with clumps of bushes and widely scattered trees. On their long legs, giraffes glide across this broad landscape with slow-motion grace, tails swishing to shoo away insects. Zebras, antelope, elephants, rhinos, and lots of smaller animals might share a giraffe's habitat, which is beautiful, wild—and dangerous.

The savanna's low hills and thickets are filled with places where predators can hide. Lions, leopards, hyenas, and African wild dogs all prey on giraffes. These predators stalk their prey, sometimes creeping for hours in the tall grass, lying just below the crest of a hill, waiting . . . waiting . . . for the perfect moment to pounce!

But a long-necked, sharp-eyed giraffe can be pretty hard to sneak up on.

Imagine if your head were six feet above your shoulders. You'd be able to see much farther than anyone around you. Giraffes' long necks rise above the tall grass like periscopes sticking up from a submarine, scanning for danger. Their

Giraffes keep a sharp lookout over the savanna.

keen eyes can spot a stalking lioness or prowling hyena before it gets close enough to pounce. Other animals, like zebras and antelope, keep a wary eye on nearby giraffes, using them as a sort of alarm system. When the giraffes start to run, so do they.

Eating up High

Leaves, leaves, and more leaves are what giraffes love to eat. Lots of other animals that live on the savanna eat leaves, too, and the bottom branches can get pretty bare. But another advantage of that super long neck is that giraffes can eat from the tops of tall trees, where no other animal can reach. Their massive bodies need a lot of food for energy, and so giraffes eat pretty much all day long. An adult giraffe can eat about seventy-five pounds of leaves in a day.

Giraffes have incredibly long tongues that are eighteen inches or more. That's about half as long as a human arm! The really weird thing about their tongues is that they're bluish-purple, and can even look black. No one knows why for sure, but perhaps the dark color helps their tongues keep from getting sunburned as the giraffes snack under the hot savanna sun. These flexible, strong tongues move like snakes, wrapping around branches and stripping off the tender leaves.

Constantly strolling from tree to tree, giraffes nibble all around, from low branches to the highest twigs. Sometimes they come eye to eye with nesting birds!

Long-necked giraffes have a bird's-eye view.

Giraffes also drink from trees, in a way. Juicy leaves give them most of the water they need. For giraffes with six-foot-long legs, lowering their head and straddling their front legs to drink from a water hole is risky. They can't quickly turn and run from predators in this awkward position, and could even break a limb. Giraffes can go for days without drinking if they have enough leaves to munch on. Every few days, though, they do need to take a drink, and then they'll take turns at the water hole, some giraffes sipping while their friends keep watch.

Gardeners of the Savanna

Giraffes are a keystone species, which is a species that is necessary to the survival of many plants and animals in its environment. Every bite giraffes take affects the savanna and its creatures—and in ways you might not expect.

Giraffes eat leaves, which you'd think would be bad for the trees. But giraffes nibble a few bites from one tree and then move on to the next—that way they don't kill any one tree by taking all its leaves. Their constant nibbling can actually help trees, because losing some leaves and stems gets them to produce strong new growth.

As giraffes sniff at a tree or bush that has flowers, they spread pollen from bloom to bloom, just like a high-flying bee might do. This pollinates the flowers so that they can produce seeds.

Once a tree produces fruit, the ever-hungry giraffes gobble up the fruit or seed pods. Then they spread the seeds in their droppings as they wander. The seeds fall to the dry ground, sur-rounded by a nice wet pile of giraffe poop. The nutrients in the giraffe droppings fertilize the seeds as they start to grow into new trees. Giraffes can travel long distances, so they carry seeds far and wide, spreading new trees to places they couldn't reach without the giraffes' help.

Without giraffes, the savanna would be more barren, with far fewer trees—a very different place.

2

FAMILIES AND FRIENDS

Giraffes really like to hang out with other giraffes. Females spend time with other females, watching over their youngsters. Some female giraffes will stay friends for years, perhaps for their whole lives. Young males will sometimes form "bachelor groups," spending time together. Meanwhile, older male giraffes, called bulls, are more likely to be loners. They move from group to group, looking for females to mate with.

Baby giraffes stay with their mothers for about a year and a half. As the young males get older, they start to wander around a lot, leaving the group and exploring on their own. Sometimes they get together with other youngsters and test each other's strength by pressing their long necks against each other, or even hitting each other with their necks. They push and shove, sort of like two kids arm wrestling. When they're old enough to mate with a female, the bulls will sometimes battle each other ferociously to win the right to mate with the females of their choice.

But wait—how do giraffes fight? They don't have claws or sharp teeth—in fact their teeth are square and flat, which is great for grinding up tough twigs and bark, but not so helpful for fighting. For a long time, people thought that giraffes were as gentle and harmless as sheep. But giraffes can be fearsome warriors. That long neck not only helps them see danger and find food, it's also a weapon. Giraffes have big, heavy heads, topped with bony spikes called ossicones. (These are why people used to think they might be unicorns!) Their muscular necks swing their heads like battering rams crashing

Giraffes can be ferocious fighters, using their heavy heads like a weapon.

into other giraffes. Giraffe battles are rarely to the death—almost always, one giraffe gives in before it's seriously injured.

The bull who wins the fight will usually mate with several of the nearby females. But then he goes off, roving across the savanna in search of a different group of females. As far as we know, giraffe babies don't spend any time hanging out with their dads.

Giraffe Kindergarten

Females with young stick especially close together. This makes sense in an environment where predators are lurking. In a group, there are more eyes to spot approaching danger. Several giraffes can band together to discourage a predator.

Because of the danger of predators, giraffes

spend a lot of time awake. Scientists used to think they rarely slept, but most of their sleeping is done standing up. It's hard to tell if a giraffe is awake or not, so we don't really know how much they sleep. Healthy adult giraffes are rarely killed by predators—a full-grown male giraffe can weigh over three thousand pounds, more than a ton and a half. That's more than some cars weigh. With one well-placed kick of its enormous hoof, which is the size of a dinner plate, a giraffe can kill a hyena or even a lion. And giraffes are fast runners, galloping about thirty-five miles an hour at top speed. They can't keep that up for long distances, but they're well able to outrun most predators as long as they get a head start.

But a baby giraffe is a different matter. Predators target young giraffes way more often than adults.

Giraffes don't breed until they are at least five years old, and a mother carries an unborn calf for fifteen months. She gives birth to one calf at a time—twins are rare. Although a newborn giraffe can walk in its first few hours of life, it staggers on clumsy, spindly legs, unable to outrun danger. When a giraffe calf is born, its mother licks and nurses it tenderly. But within a few hours of the birth, the mother leaves the baby and strolls away, often not returning for hours. Biologists used to be convinced that giraffes were unattached, careless mothers.

But leaving the baby is actually the best way to protect it. The well-fed infant is securely hidden in the tall grass. The calf lies very still, and the tan blotches on its fur provide good camouflage among the tall brown clumps of grass. Predators aren't likely to notice the hidden, helpless young one. The mother forages for food miles away, returning only once or twice in a day to nurse the baby on high-energy milk. Many other mammals, including white-tailed deer, rabbits, and cows, use this hiding strategy, too. (That's why you might find a fawn or a nest of baby cottontails in your backyard, with no mother in sight.)

Baby giraffes grow quickly, as much as a couple of inches a day. (Imagine if human infants did that!) After just a few days, as soon as the youngsters are good at running around, they join their mother and other females with young. Then the calves go to what one biologist called "giraffe kindergarten."

A Colombian zoology student named Carlos Mejia was one of the first zoologists to question the idea that giraffes were bad mothers.

Giraffes are loving mothers.

Working with the Serengeti Research Institute in Tanzania, he spent thousands of hours observing giraffes in the wild and learned to recognize many of them by the patterns of blotches on their fur. After patiently following female giraffes around for weeks at a time, he realized that what seemed to be careless abandonment was actually a social network in action.

Mother giraffes lead their babies to a grassy hill, from which there are good views of possible predators. One female giraffe stays with the calves while the other mothers travel long distances to feed. This system lets the mothers go in search of the nutrition their bodies need to produce milk to feed their babies. They take turns being on guard and seeking out thickets and groves with lots of leaves to eat.

Just like kids in a kindergarten classroom, the young giraffes are learning all sorts of new things. They sniff and lick each other, making new friends. They race around and shove each other playfully, experiment with nibbling new foods, and then take a nap in the shade—all under the watchful eye of the adult in charge.

Far from being careless mothers, giraffe females protect their young fiercely. Carlos watched a lone female defend her baby from a hungry lion, driving it off with a flurry of well-placed, powerful kicks.

A Little Night Music

On a moonlit night, many sounds drift across the dark savanna. You might hear the chirp of insects, the laughing howl of a hyena, or the deep, chesty roar of a lion. And if you listen closely, you might be able to hear the song of the giraffes.

What kinds of noises do giraffes make? Males sometimes make a sort of coughing sound, especially when trying to get the attention of females. Mothers will snort or grunt to alert their young of danger. But for centuries, people thought that giraffes were voiceless creatures, assuming that their extremely long necks made it impossible for them to use their vocal cords.

In 2015, a team of wildlife researchers wanted to find out more about giraffe communication. Using highly sensitive microphones, they recorded several different groups of zoo giraffes, monitoring every sound they made twenty-four hours a day. And they made an astonishing discovery: in the dark, the giraffes were humming.

Each group of giraffes produced a deep, musical humming. The low sound rose and fell, on and on through the darkness, as the animals almost seemed to be harmonizing with each other. These sounds have only been recorded at night.

Why did the giraffes hum together—but only after dark? Perhaps it's a way to keep the herd together on dark nights when, in the wild,

Humming together in the moonlight.

a lone giraffe far from the group could end up as a predator's dinner. Perhaps it's an identification call, a way of saying "Here I am!" Do all giraffes do this, or only some of the ones in zoos? Scientists have many theories, but no one knows for sure.

Giraffes also communicate in ways other than sound, and biologists are only beginning to figure out how giraffes send messages to each other. Giraffes' sharp eyes can spot little head bobs or ear twitches that humans hardly notice but that may have a lot of meaning to another giraffe. Watching a mother giraffe lick and nuzzle a newborn, we can clearly see they communicate by touch as well.

F008

In 2010, a biologist named Zoe Muller was studying giraffes on a wildlife preserve in Kenya. As she began to recognize individual animals, she gave them names so she could keep track of them. One female had a calf that had been born with a malformed leg and was unable to walk far. Zoe named the mother F008, as it was the eighth female she had identified.

Unlike the other mothers who often moved

away from their young, F008 rarely left her youngster's side. Then one day, Zoe observed that the calf was lying motionless in the grass, and she realized that it had died. As F008 stood over her baby, other females began to approach. More than a dozen gathered around, and Zoe never forgot what she saw then. "I observed the adult females [including F008] approaching the carcass and 'nudging' it with their muzzles, then lifting their heads to look around before bending down to nudge it again," she remembered. Many giraffes stood around the body all day and on through the night. When the sun rose over the savanna the next morning, they were still there.

On the third day, the other females began to leave, one by one. But F008 remained near her calf's body, not eating or drinking, for five days.

We can never look inside an animal's mind and know what it's thinking, and of course, we can't know what emotions a giraffe might possibly feel. Was F008 mourning the death of her little one? Were the others trying to comfort her? We'll never know for sure, but the more we learn about giraffes, the more we realize how strong their connections are to their families and friends.

One Giraffe, or Nine Giraffes?

If you look at several giraffes in a zoo, they look pretty much alike at first. But if you start looking more closely, you might notice that the patterns of blotches covering their bodies are different. Some are chocolate brown with a network of thin white lines. Others have pale beige spots with big patches of white in between. Are they just different color varieties, like Labrador retrievers that are brown and yellow? Or are the differences more than skin-deep? Scientists have long been debating exactly how many kinds of giraffes there are.

At first, zoologists thought that there was just one species of giraffe with as many as nine subspecies. A subspecies is a group that doesn't interbreed with another group in the wild, although it could if they were brought together in a zoo.

Now, with the development of complex microscopes and other tools, scientists have the ability to look deep into animals' cells and examine their DNA. Most scientists agree new research shows that there is more than one species of giraffe.

Some species, like reticulated giraffes and

Maasai giraffes, live in ranges that are within a few miles of each other, yet they don't interbreed. These groups are no more closely related to each other than, say, a brown bear is to a polar bear.

But does it really matter how closely a northern giraffe is related to a southern giraffe? For many years, no one except a few zoologists really cared if there were nine different species of giraffes, or four, or only one. But now in the twenty-first century, the question of how to classify giraffe species has become a matter of life and death.

How Many Giraffes?

How many giraffes are there? That's a hard question to answer. Giraffes roam over remote areas in many different African countries, and it's difficult to get an exact count of their population. Scientists estimate that there are approximately 100,000 giraffes in the wild today.

This big number makes it seem that giraffes are doing pretty well. Lions, for example, have only about 35,000 individual animals remaining. But the numbers are deceiving. If the total giraffe population is made up of several different species that do not interbreed, then that changes everything.

Now we're realizing that each species of giraffe needs to be considered separately from the others. And that makes the numbers look a lot scarier. Reticulated giraffes, for instance, are down to approximately 15,000 animals, and some researchers think it may be as low as 9,000. The question of how to classify giraffes is getting more and more urgent—because giraffe population numbers have taken a shocking dive in recent years.

Once, vast herds of giraffes lived on the wild, open lands of the African subcontinent (the part below the Sahara). There were more than a million giraffes in the 1700s. But then their numbers began to sink, decreasing year after year.

Giraffes are one of the most popular animals in the world. We see them on TV, in commercials, on greeting cards, on the pages of calendars and books. There are giraffe puppets, giraffe stuffed toys, lovable giraffe cartoon characters. It seems as though giraffes have always been around—and always will be.

But could there come a time when no more of the long-necked giants roam the African savanna?

3

WHY ARE GIRAFFES IN TROUBLE?

All over the world, countless animals, plants, and fungi are at risk of completely disappearing. The International Union for Conservation of Nature keeps a careful inventory, known as the IUCN Red List of Threatened Species™, of all the threatened species in the world. There are different categories: Least Concern, Near Threatened, and Vulnerable mean that a species is at some risk. Endangered means that its population in the wild is so low that a species is in grave danger. Critically Endangered means the species is at even greater risk. Extinct in the Wild means that the creature still exists in zoos, so that there is the hope of returning the animal to its natural habitat someday. Extinct is the last category—that means the species has disappeared from the planet forever.

In the 1980s, there were approximately 150,000 giraffes in the wild. The populations seemed stable, and little was being done to study them. Few people, even among wildlife biologists, really noticed that giraffe numbers were slowly but steadily dropping. Other species, like elephants, lions, and rhinos, got more attention, more publicity in the international press for their dwindling numbers, and more funding to try to save them. For many years, giraffes were listed on the Red List as Least Concern.

And then as the twenty-first century dawned, new research techniques made it easier to identify and study giraffes, and to figure out how many there were. Suddenly scientists realized— giraffes were in trouble! In 2016, giraffes (all species lumped together) were uplisted, which means that their numbers had fallen so low that their status had to be changed to the much more worrying Vulnerable.

Why are giraffe numbers dropping so low, so fast? What's going on?

Shrinking Habitat

More and bigger cities connected by more and longer roads can bring opportunities for people. But developing a country's resources often means more pressure on nature and wild animals.

Giraffes find food by traveling from place

The giraffes' wild world is getting smaller.

to place, often covering many miles in a single day. They'll head to one area when rains have greened up the trees, and then move to another place with different plants to eat as the dry weather sets in. Once, giraffes roamed over millions of acres of open savanna. But every year, more and more people are taking over spaces giraffes used to use.

Some giraffe territory holds valuable minerals or oil. Digging these up can bring in a lot of money. Other areas of giraffe habitat are destroyed when people cut trees to use for firewood or for making charcoal to burn for fuel. Also, people need to use land to grow food: crops like corn or sweet potatoes.

In the past, small farms were scattered across the landscape in many countries where giraffes lived, with herds of goats or cattle grazing on the savanna. Farmers living in this traditional manner, called pastoralists, could share space with giraffes. Often giraffes would peacefully nibble leaves within sight of villages and crop fields. Researchers found that giraffe babies often had a better rate of survival when they grew up closer to the pastoral farms, perhaps because farmers kept away lions and other predators.

Modern farms, in contrast, tend to be like big factories, taking up thousands of acres of land. Huge crop fields cover land that was once savanna. The plants that grow wild on the dry savanna have long, tough roots that sink deep into the ground to reach water. These strong roots help hold the soil in place when big rains come. But when native plants are replaced with short-rooted crops, the soil erodes and crumbles away.

Cows are also a big problem for giraffes. Mega-farms may have tens of thousands of cattle on land where giraffes used to live. The hungry cattle devour not only grass but also young tree seedlings, leaving no new trees able to sprout. In times of drought, livestock use up the scarce water. Also, giraffes may not look much like cows, but they're both hoofed animals with similar bodies on the inside. Cows can carry diseases like anthrax that are deadly for giraffes.

Most African countries have national parks or preserves for wildlife to live on. But more and more, these areas are getting separated from each other by highways, farms, and towns. Giraffes sometimes get hit by cars or trains, or become tangled in power lines strung across lands where they used to roam freely. When habitat is broken up like this, it's called habitat fragmentation, and it's very hard on wildlife, especially animals like giraffes that roam many miles.

Troubled Times

Giraffes don't pay attention to boundaries

between countries. But the continent of Africa is made up of more than fifty different nations. People in these countries don't all speak the same languages or have the same cultures or traditions. Some nations have stable governments, which can support public parks and national wildlife preserves and can pay staffs of park rangers to protect animals. Others are undergoing painful periods of disruption and conflict, for people and wildlife.

Angola was a nation with many parks and preserves that were home to a type of giraffe called the Angolan giraffe. But when a deadly civil war broke out in the country in the 1970s, more than a million people were killed, and millions more fled from their homes. Starving people took refuge in parks and wildlife preserves, killing wild animals for food. The war dragged on from the 1960s until it finally ended in 2002. Angolan giraffes were all but exterminated in their homeland, although they survive in other countries.

The Most Dangerous Predator

Giraffes are hunted by many species, but their most dangerous predator is humans. In ancient times, African hunters killed giraffes with spears, bows and arrows, or traps called snares. The hunter-gatherers used almost every part of the animals they hunted—not only the nutritious meat, but also tough, string-like tendons for bowstrings and rope, and skins for clothing or for making leather shields for protection in battle. The huge giraffe herds, with plenty of habitat available, weren't badly affected by this kind of hunting.

Now with giraffes struggling with ever-shrinking habitats, most species are so scarce that it's illegal to hunt them. (Only South African, also known as southern, giraffes can be legally hunted.) But hunting that's against the law, called poaching, is a constant threat. Wild animals are often used as a cheap source of food. Poachers sell this low-cost "bushmeat" to people who can't afford other forms of meat. Sometimes poachers hunt giraffes by shooting them, but often they set snares, to wrap tightly around the giraffe's neck or foot. Even if the giraffe escapes, these can cause painful injuries or death.

Buying and Selling Giraffes

People hunt giraffes for reasons other than food, too. It was a big win for wildlife conservation when the use of elephant ivory (made from elephants' tusks) was banned in almost all the nations of the world. But sadly the massive bones of giraffes often take the place of elephant ivory for knife handles, carvings, and other items. Giraffe bones bring a high price. So do giraffe pelts, tails, and other body parts. Dealers sell giraffe-skin rugs, giraffe-tail fly whisks, giraffe-hide boots, and many other products made from giraffe bodies.

Rare animals like giant pandas and gorillas are protected by CITES, the Convention on International Trade in Endangered Species. This is an agreement among the governments of more than 180 different nations to control the trade of wild specimens so that the survival of animal or plant species isn't threatened. It protects live animals as well as products made from their bodies. But before people had realized giraffe numbers were dropping, giraffes were not officially listed as endangered by CITES, so they weren't protected as the trade in giraffe parts increased.

Changing Climate

Another problem for giraffes is one that has tremendous effects on people, too. Human-caused pollution has changed Earth's atmosphere and caused temperatures to rise. The African savanna has never been an easy place to live, but the increased heat and droughts caused by climate change make it even harder for giraffes to survive.

Without the life-giving rains that come once or twice a year, grass on the savanna becomes more and more sparse, and trees shrivel. Treeless, shadeless deserts are not habitats that can support healthy populations of giraffes. Giraffes need large numbers of trees to eat, and giraffe calves depend on trees for shade and shelter from predators.

But sometimes the problem facing giraffes isn't too little rain—it's too much. Climate change also causes increased hurricanes, storms, and floods. Torrential rains wash away trees, erode soil, and destroy giraffe habitats. Climate change affects every living thing on our planct, and giraffes are already feeling its effects.

Let's Get Loud!

Giraffes have completely vanished from at least seven African countries where there used to be tens of thousands. But still they don't seem to get as much attention as species like ele-

*As our climate changes,
the giraffes' habitat is changing, too.*

phants and rhinos. Many people aren't aware that giraffes are in trouble. Because the decline in giraffe populations isn't getting the publicity and headlines that some other species attract, biologists are calling it "the silent extinction."

So it's up to people who care about giraffes (like you) to stop the silent extinction—by making a lot of noise!

4

GIVING GIRAFFES A VOICE

When Zoe Muller observed F008 watching over her calf, she realized that this was a powerful story—a way of shouting out loud about the silent extinction. She spread the word, and F008's story was told again and again, in newspapers, blog posts, and social media. The giraffe mother who refused to leave her baby touched the hearts of people around the world. F008's fame helped wake the world up to the danger of losing wild giraffes.

Keeping an Eye on Giraffes

But as the efforts to protect giraffes picked up, people began to realize something surprising: how much we *don't* know about giraffes. In order to save any endangered species, we need to know a lot about them. How much land do giraffes need to find food? Where do they have their babies? What happens if you move a giraffe to a new habitat?

Giraffes don't sit around in one place. They wander territories covering hundreds of square miles, across roadless savannas. How could biologists observe what they do, and where they do it— without following the animals so closely that

Giraffes are looking to us for help.

they're frightened or stressed? As giraffes were uplisted to Vulnerable, people in Africa and around the world got busy solving this problem.

My Spots Are Different than Your Spots

Just as no two people have the same fingerprints, no two giraffes have exactly the same pattern of blotches on their fur. This fun fact turns out to be really important for researchers. Scientists can use these patterns to recognize individual animals and keep track of where they go.

In a recent study of giraffes in Tanzania by an organization called Wild Nature Institute, researchers photographed almost three thousand Maasai giraffes and identified them by their spot patterns. Then they kept track of the giraffes year after year, watching as the animals moved from place to place, found food, avoided

Researchers can identify individual giraffes by the pattern of the blotches on their fur.

predators, and made friends. They also kept careful count of how many babies were born and how many survived their first year.

The researchers found that female giraffes live with of dozens of other females in close-knit groups that biologist Dr. Derek Lee calls "girl gangs"—and the gangs don't mix. "Gang membership was pretty tight," he says. "Even though members of different girl gangs often spent time in the same areas, members of different communities rarely interacted with each other."

Some girl gangs have more calves survive than other groups do, even if they live in the same habitat. Now scientists are trying to figure out why. Maybe some of the girl gangs are fiercer at fending off predators. Or maybe they're better at finding the most nutritious food.

Because very young giraffes are the most likely to be caught by predators, many baby giraffes don't survive their first year. It takes a long time for giraffe populations to rebound from losses. So finding ways to help calves survive is especially important.

The more we know about giraffes, the better we can plan ways to help them.

Guarding Giraffes

Symon Masiaine, a member of the Maasai community, grew up in a village close to Loisaba Conservancy, a nature preserve in Kenya. "There have been a lot of changes," he says sadly. "When I was growing up, there were a lot of giraffes in this area. Now there aren't many." Symon joined the Twiga Walinzi to help protect the animals he loves.

Twiga is the word for "giraffe" in Kiswahili, a language spoken in many African countries, and Twiga Walinzi means "Giraffe Guards." The San Diego Zoo, Giraffe Conservation Foundation, and other organizations worked together with people in communities near where giraffes live to form this team. The Twiga Walinzi patrol the land, not only national parks but also grazing lands and farms outside

Ranger Mike Parkei is one of many men and women working to protect wild giraffes.

the protected areas. They keep watch for poachers, help injured giraffes, and remove thousands of wire snares. Ruth Lekupanae, one of the Twiga Walinzi, knows firsthand how sad it is to see giraffes with wounds from wire snares on their bodies. "We need to work with the communities in this area to tell people that the animals belong to us," she says. "It is our responsibility to protect them."

The Giraffe Guards also set up and maintain a vast network of a hundred motion-sensor cameras across two conservation areas in Kenya. These special cameras take a picture of anything in front of them that moves. In a year, the cameras might take more than a million images, and only a few thousand of the photos will be of giraffes. Hundreds of volunteers from all over the world log on to a website where they can look over the images to help figure out what's in them.

Living with Giraffes

As more and more people move into giraffe territory, human needs and giraffe needs bump into each other. What do you do when a three-thousand-pound giraffe turns up in your backyard?

How does a farmer keep a giraffe out of their crop fields, or persuade cows and giraffes to share a water hole? What should you do when a giraffe wants to cross a road? Lots of organizations are working to help farmers and other people figure out ways that cows, humans, and giraffes can share living space. They're also helping kids in Africa learn about giraffes and ways to protect them.

The Giraffe Conservation Foundation sponsors a series of programs called Twiga Wetu, which means "Our Giraffe." Twiga Wetu staff do a wide range of educational programs for kids and adults in countries like Niger, Uganda, and Namibia.

Wild Nature Institute works with students in Tanzania, using a book about a character named Juma the Giraffe and an education program called Celebrating Africa's Giants. They also help students plant trees to create better habitats.

An organization called the Reticulated Giraffe Project partners with the rangers of the Samburu National Reserve in Kenya. Students board the Dala Dala Wa Twiga—the "Giraffe Bus"—to take a trip to the reserve to see giraffes in the wild. (Now that sounds like a pretty good field trip!)

The First "Giraffologist"

A kid who meets a giraffe might grow up to be a wildlife biologist who studies and helps giraffes. A young girl named Anne Innis Dagg glimpsed her first giraffe in a Canadian zoo. She was spellbound by the awesome animal and found she never could forget it. In 1956, after getting a degree in biology, Anne made a solo journey to South Africa. She became the first scientist in the world to study giraffes in the wild. For more than fifty years, Anne has written books, taught students, and fought to protect wildlife, always remembering that first experience of looking a living giraffe in the eyes.

The power of seeing a live animal can change people's lives. And since most people can't make a trip to see giraffes in their natural home, zoos are the next best option.

Giraffes are hard to take care of in captivity. Long-legged giraffes must have plenty of space to move around in. They also need specially designed indoor enclosures with high roofs so they don't bump their heads! And it's really important that they be kept warm. Giraffes don't mind heat, but if the temperature drops

Dr. Anne Innis Dagg, the first giraffologist.

much below 50 degrees Fahrenheit, they're in danger of dying from the cold. And zookeepers are realizing that, just like people, giraffes can't thrive without a community of family and friends.

But there are some really good things about zoos. If the worst should happen and giraffes become extinct in the wild, at least there will be a wide network of giraffes in zoos all over the world, so that they could someday be replaced in their natural habitat. And many zoos support conservation all over the world, helping to save wild places.

Internet Rock Star

Hundreds of people might visit a giraffe in a zoo. But with the growing power of social media, one zoo giraffe can touch millions of people's hearts.

April was one of the reticulated giraffes at a small New York zoo called Animal Adventure Park, and in 2017, she was expecting a baby. The zoo staff put a live cam in her pen and shared news of the upcoming birth on social media.

Soon they were astonished to find their post had gone viral. Thousands—then hundreds of thousands—then *millions* of people waited anxiously for April's baby to be born.

An estimated 1.2 million people watched the birth on live stream and were thrilled when the infant giraffe finally arrived; a knobby-kneed baby, with big brown eyes and huge ears, he weighed 129 pounds and was five feet, nine inches tall at birth. Allysa Swilley, one of the zoo staff, named him Tajiri, from the Kiswahili word for hope.

April and her baby became an internet sensation, with more than 230 million views on Animal Adventure Park's YouTube feed. Because of April, millions of people around the world were inspired to care about the future of giraffes. "Hope is not only something that

Tajiri has brought to you guys as a community globally, but a hope for giraffes," says Allysa. "We have been able to give giraffes a voice."

Working to Help Giraffes

Giraffes face tough times ahead. Some populations are holding steady or even increasing, but others are struggling. Giraffes as a whole are still listed as Vulnerable on the Red List, but in 2018, Kordofan giraffes and Nubian giraffes, which the IUCN considers subspecies, were officially listed as Critically Endangered, while reticulated giraffes were uplisted to Endangered. Maasai giraffes are also considered Endangered.

Giraffes got some good news in 2019, when several African nations including the Central African Republic, Chad, Kenya, Mali, Niger, and Senegal joined together to propose that giraffes of all species be added to the list of animals protected by CITES, the international treaty that controls the buying and selling of wildlife. Now at last there are laws to limit the international trade in giraffe body parts.

Many conservation groups are urging that giraffes be listed as Endangered under the US Endangered Species Act. That would make it illegal to buy or sell giraffe body parts in all fifty states.

Giraffes in zoos around the world will keep on teaching people why they should care about wildlife conservation. Meanwhile, African governments and many global organizations are working to do the same in the field, where giraffes live in the wild. They sponsor training programs for park rangers, rapid response teams to stop poachers, and care centers for injured or orphaned giraffes.

Sometimes giraffes threatened by drought or habitat loss are moved to a new place. But the more we learn about giraffes, the more we realize how complicated and important their social connections are. Just like it's hard to be the new kid in school, it's stressful for giraffes to make new friends and get used to a new area.

And the more we learn about how far giraffes roam from place to place, the more urgent is the need to save millions of acres of habitat for these long-legged wanderers to thrive. Scientists are working with the governments of several African countries to set up protected routes called critical linkage zones. These help giraffes travel safely between feeding areas, avoiding the dangers of towns, power lines, and roads.

All across Africa, researchers are keeping an eye on giraffes, carefully monitoring which groups are in trouble and which ones are doing well. Sometimes, it's possible to respond to situations where giraffes need help—fast. In 2020, a herd of giraffes in Kenya were facing a disaster that presented a tough challenge for the people trying to help them: How do you put a giraffe in a boat?

Stuck in the Mud

For many years, a small herd of Rothschild's giraffes had lived on Longicharo Island in Kenya's Lake Baringo. But pounding rainstorms had turned the land they lived on into a muddy swamp. No food was left—and the water was rising! The giraffes were in trouble.

People living nearby worked with organizations like Save Giraffes Now to make a rescue plan to float the giraffes to safety. Carpenters from the nearby Pokot and Njemps villages designed a flat-bottomed barge, strong enough to carry more than a ton of weight. They christened the boat the GiRaft.

Asiwa was a female giraffe isolated on a section of island that was eroding fast. With barely an acre left to forage in, she had to be rescued first. Asiwa was briefly tranquilized while a blindfold was placed over her eyes and guide ropes were attached to her neck and shoulders. Then she was led toward the water as rescuers watched anxiously. How would she react?

David O'Connor of Save Giraffes Now was one of the main organizers of the rescue. "She was incredible," he remembered. "She's a very, very tough girl." The team held their

The GiRaft in action!

breath as Asiwa approached the raft, but she didn't hesitate.

The raft was towed by motorboat out into deep, crocodile-filled waters while a dozen canoes with helpers paddled alongside. The giraffe stood still, her hooded head sticking out above the raft's high side walls. The ride lasted more than an hour, but Asiwa remained calm and landed safely.

It took months to rescue all the animals, but finally the last two giraffes were rafted to safety. Spectators clapped and cheered as Ngarikoni and her three-month-old calf, Noelle, stepped off the raft and entered their new home, a 44,000-acre preserve called the Ruko Conservancy. The long-term goal is to introduce more and more giraffes into Ruko, and build a healthy population that can expand from the conservancy. Perhaps someday giraffes will return to places where they used to live, like Kenya's Eastern Rift Valley.

"We knew we had to come together and do everything possible to save them," said Mike Parkei, a ranger at the preserve. "Giraffes are the heart of our homeland."

With so many people working hard to help giraffes, and many voices uplifted to protect them, there is hope that giraffes will avoid the silent extinction. There's hope that the long-legged giants will continue striding over the savanna, gazing with their keen eyes across the wilds of Africa—and humming in the moonlight.

What lies ahead for giraffes?

FUN FACTS ABOUT GIRAFFES

1. Giraffes have had very long necks for a very long time. Biologists think that giraffes have had their extreme necks as part of their bodies since at least seven million years ago.

2. Even though giraffes have the longest necks of any mammal, they can't easily eat grass—because they can't reach it! Their necks are too short for their heads to touch the ground. To reach down, or to take a drink, they have to splay their super long front legs in an awkward

position, or bend their knees.

3. Giraffes have a lot of heart. An adult giraffe's heart weighs more than twenty-five pounds and is about two feet long. (Your heart is a lot smaller—it's about the size of your fist.) They need a big, strong heart to pump blood all the way up that long neck.

4. Full-grown giraffes are among the heaviest land mammals. Only elephants, rhinos, and hippos weigh more.

5. The smallest adult giraffe ever seen in the wild was recently spotted in Namibia. Researchers have named him Nigel, and he's about eight feet high—taller than the tallest basketball players, although a lot shorter than most adult giraffes.

6. In the wild, giraffes need to stay on the

alert for predators. They spend most of their lives standing up, because it's difficult for them to get up in a hurry. They can even sleep standing up.

7. Giraffes have the largest eyes of any land mammal. Unlike many types of animals, they can see in color.

8. Both male and female giraffes have ossicones sticking out of the tops of their skulls. Females' ossicones are thin and tufted with hair, but the males' ossicones are thicker and often bald on top.

9. Giraffes have seven neck bones called cervical vertebrae. That's the same number of neck bones as humans have—the giraffe bones are just really long and thick.

HOW YOU CAN HELP SAVE THE GIRAFFES

Help stop the silent extinction by getting LOUD about giraffes.

1. Do a science fair project, start a school environmental club, or consider working with an adult to use social media to spread the word about giraffes.

2. Use your birthday or other holidays to ask friends and family to donate to one of the not-for-profit organizations that work to help giraffes:

- Anne Innis Dagg Foundation:
  AnneInnisDaggFoundation.org
- Giraffe Conservation Foundation:
  GiraffeConservation.org
- Northern Rangelands Trust:
  NRT-Kenya.org
- Save Giraffes Now:
  SaveGiraffesNow.org
- Wild Nature Institute:
  WildNatureInstitute.org

3. Adopt a giraffe! No, you can't bring it home—it wouldn't fit in your house anyway—but some not-for-profits, including the Giraffe Conservation Foundation, Wild Nature Institute, and World Wildlife Fund, offer symbolic adoption programs.

4. Join the Junior Giraffe Club. The Anne

Innis Dagg Foundation sponsors a free club for young people aged seven to seventeen, with online meetings where you can talk with field scientists as well as other kids all over the world. JuniorGiraffeClub.org.

5. World Giraffe Day is easy to remember— June 21: the longest day of the year (in the Northern Hemisphere) for the creature with the longest neck.

6. If you go to a zoo, make sure it's giraffe friendly. Check out the zoo and make sure it's a not-for-profit organization that takes excellent care of its animals and supports conservation activities in wild giraffe habitats. If you visit a place where you believe the giraffes are not well cared for, consider getting involved

by contacting animal welfare authorities. Look for zoos that are accredited by the Association of Zoos and Aquariums (AZA) as having the highest standards of animal care: AZA.org.

7. Help the Twiga Walinzi! Visit the Wildwatch Kenya website run by the San Diego Zoo to learn how you can view online photos taken by motion-sensor cameras set up by the Giraffe Guards, and help classify the images in the photos: Zooniverse.org/Projects/ SanDiegoZooGlobal/Wildwatch-Kenya.

8. Speak out against the trade in giraffe parts! Write to your representatives in Congress and make it clear that you want them to take strong action on protecting endangered species, especially

giraffes. Contact federal officials to push for national protections for giraffes, and contact state officials, too. In 2019, New York State became the first state to pass a law banning the sale of giraffe parts.

9. VOTE! Until you're old enough to vote yourself, support political candidates who support environmental protection. Encourage your family and friends to vote with the environment in mind.

ACKNOWLEDGMENTS

Grateful thanks to the all the dedicated giraffe researchers and guardians who are helping to save these magnificent animals.

Special thanks to the experts who shared their knowledge and reviewed the manuscript:

- Stephanie Fennessy of Giraffe Conservation Foundation
- Monica Bond of Wild Nature Institute
- David O'Connor of Save Giraffes Now

Many thanks to Save Giraffes Now, Wild Nature Institute, and the Anne Innis Dagg Foundation for providing photographs.

REFERENCES

Almond, Kyle. "Giraffes Are Stuck on a Flooding Island. But the Rescues Have Begun." Photographs by Ami Vitale. CNN, December 2020. https://www.cnn.com /interactive/2020/12/world/giraffe-rescue -kenya-cnnphotos/index.html.

Anderson, Tanya. *Giraffe Extinction: Using Science and Technology to Save the Gentle Giants.* Minneapolis, MN: Twenty-First Century Books, 2020.

Bond, Monica. "Giraffe Social Communities Are Important to Giraffe Populations."

PopEcol. Population Ecology Research Group at the University of Zurich, April 8, 2021. http://www.popecol.org /giraffe-social-communities-are-important -to-giraffe-populations/.

Dagg, Anne Innis. *5 Giraffes*. Markham, ON: Fitzhenry and Whiteside, 2016.

Dagg, Anne Innis. *Giraffe: Biology, Behaviour and Conservation*. Cambridge: Cambridge University Press, 2019.

Hamutenya, Jackson. "Can We Take the Angolan Giraffe Back to Angola?" Conservation Namibia, July 27, 2021. https://conservationnamibia.com/blog /b2021-angolan-giraffe.php.

"Moment When Baby Giraffe and Mother Are Rescued from a Flooded Kenya Island." Today UK News, April 12, 2021.

https://todayuknews.com/science
/moment-when-baby-giraffe-and-mother
-are-rescued-from-a-flooded-kenya
-island/.

Muller, Zoe, and Stephen Harris. "A Review
of the Social Behaviour of the Giraffe
Giraffa camelopardalis: A Misunderstood
but Socially Complex Species." *Mammal
Review* 52, no. 1 (August 2, 2021): 1–15.
https://doi.org/10.1111/mam.12268.

Northern Rangelands Trust. "Community
Conservation." Accessed 2021.
https://www.nrt-kenya.org/community
-conservation-overview.

"Research and Protection of Masai Giraffes."
Wild Nature Institute. Accessed 2021.
https://www.wildnatureinstitute.org
/giraffe.html.

Reticulated Giraffe Project. Accessed 2021.
http://www.reticulatedgiraffeproject.net
/en/RGP-Home.html.

Russo, Christina M. "What You Don't
Know about Giraffes Might Move You
to Tears." The Dodo, May 28, 2015.
https://www.thedodo.com/giraffe
-mothers-conservation-1170369798.html.

Save Giraffes Now. "Save Giraffes Now
Projects." Accessed 2021.
https://savegiraffesnow.org/
projects-overview/.

Shorrocks, Brian. *The Giraffe: Biology, Ecology,
Evolution and Behaviour*. Chichester, UK:
Wiley Blackwell, 2016.

Stacy-Dawes, Jenna, and Ruth Lekupanae.
"Uganda Be Kidding Me!" *Science Blog.*
San Diego Zoo Wildlife Alliance, April 13,

2020. https://science.sandiegozoo.org
/science-blog/uganda-be-kidding-me.

"Twiga Tracker: Largest GPS Satellite
Tracking Study Ever Conducted on
Giraffe." EarthRanger, April 7, 2021.
https://www.earthranger.com/success
-stories/twiga-tracker-largest-gps
-satellite-tracking-study.

"Where Do Giraffe Move?" Giraffe
Conservation Foundation, April 7, 2021.
https://giraffeconservation.org
/2021/04/07/giraffe-movements/.

ANITA SANCHEZ is especially fascinated by plants and animals that no one loves and by the unusual, often ignored wild places of the world. Her award-winning books sing the praises of the unappreciated: dandelions, poison ivy, tarantulas, mud puddles. Her goal is to make young readers excited about science and nature. Many years of field work and teaching outdoor classes have given her firsthand experience in introducing students to the wonders of the natural world.

Photo by George Steele

You can visit Anita Sanchez online at
AnitaSanchez.com
and follow her on Twitter
@ASanchezAuthor

CHELSEA CLINTON is the author of the #1 *New York Times* bestseller *She Persisted: 13 American Women Who Changed the World*; *She Persisted Around the World: 13 Women Who Changed History*; *She Persisted in Sports: American Olympians Who Changed the Game*; *Don't Let Them Disappear: 12 Endangered Species Across the Globe*; *It's Your World: Get Informed, Get Inspired & Get Going!*; *Start Now!: You Can Make a Difference*; with Hillary Clinton, *Grandma's Gardens* and *The Book of Gutsy Women: Favorite Stories of Courage and Resilience*; and, with Devi Sridhar, *Governing Global Health: Who Runs the World and Why?* She is also the Vice Chair of the Clinton Foundation, where she works on many initiatives, including those that help empower the next generation of leaders. She lives in New York City with her husband, Marc, their children and their dog, Soren.

Photo courtesy of the author

You can follow Chelsea Clinton on Twitter
@ChelseaClinton
or on Facebook at
Facebook.com/ChelseaClinton

DON'T MISS MORE BOOKS IN THE

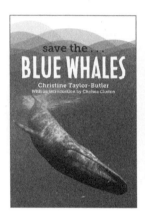

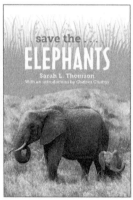

save the... SERIES!

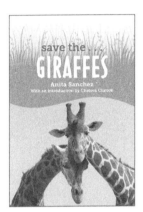

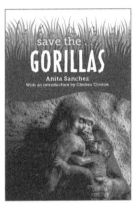

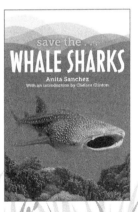